Published by
Grandreams Limited
435-437 Edgware Road, Little Venice
London W2 1TH

Printed in Malaysia

50
BEDTIME
STORIES

Written by Anne McKie
Illustrated by Ken McKie

Contents

Maggie Keeps Quiet

Maggie was a little girl who made a lot of noise.

You could hear her shouting all over the house and right down the road. In fact, Maggie's voice was so loud, everyone in the town could hear her.

One day her Nana sent her a present... 'The Little Hairdresser's Kit,'

Her toys were pleased. Her pets were thrilled, and her mum was delighted.

"The Little Hairdresser's Kit will keep her quiet for a while," everyone agreed.

"We can but hope!" said her dad in a whisper.

When Maggie opened her present, it was full of combs and grips and rollers and pins, as well as a pair of very safe scissors!

For the rest of that day, Maggie was totally silent. All you could hear (if you really listened hard) was the snip, snip, snip, of the very safe scissors, and the quiet pfffft, pfffft, of hairspray.

"I've finished," said Maggie softly as she opened her bedroom door.

It was Mum's turn to scream! It was Dad's turn to shout! The toys and the pets made so much noise...you could hear them all over the house, right down the road. In fact, everyone in the town could hear them!

Skip's Springs

Skip the hare had very long legs. He could hop so far and jump so high and run so fast, that no-one could keep up with him.

Nobody ever went for a walk with Skip, or jogged, or went on a cross-country run with him, because he always left everyone far behind.

So Skip sat at home all alone feeling very sorry for himself.

One day as he sat by himself, his favourite chair fell to pieces and all the springs popped out!

Did this worry Skip? Not one bit...it gave him a wonderful idea! Now his friends have no trouble keeping up with Skip at all!

9

Paddy's Helpers

Paddy the Park-keeper sat down on a grassy bank in his park and mopped his brow.

"The west wind was blowing hard last night. It blew the litter baskets over and scattered paper all round my nice clean park."

And Paddy mopped his brow again.

"I've been picking up litter all day long. My back aches and I'm hot and tired!"

Now the hedgehog family happened to be playing hide and seek under the bushes. They heard what Paddy the Park-keeper said, and they felt sorry for him.

"We'll have all this paper picked up in a jiffy, and have some fun at the same time!" giggled the oldest hedgehog.

Very soon all the little hedgehogs began to roll over and over and over, squealing and laughing. The paper stuck to their prickles, and the litter in the park was cleared up in next to no time.

Paddy was delighted, the hedgehog family had a great time and were each given a strawberry ice-cream as a reward!

Big Ben Comes To Help

One morning early in the summer, a long articulated lorry drove through the farmyard gate.

On the back trailer were lots of big packing cases. The Little Green Tractor wondered what they could be.

So the Little Green Tractor started up his engine and helped the lorry driver unload all those mysterious packing cases.

"I'm far too busy baling hay this morning," the farmer told his son Willie. "You'd better take a look inside!"

Now when Willie opened the first packing case, he guessed at once what was inside.

Straightaway he rang his girlfriend Tessa, who was a mechanic, and he asked her to come over as quickly as she could.

"We shall need a bit of help," said Willie to the Little Green Tractor as they rolled a giant wheel across the farmyard.

Everyone worked hard, and soon all the packing cases were empty, and the yard was full of lots of bits and pieces of an enormous machine.

It didn't take Willie and Tessa too long to put it all together, because they had a book that told you how, and lots of special spanners.

The Little Green Tractor helped too, of course!

"Well I never!" yelled the farmer from the hay field. "That's my new Giant Tractor - I quite forgot I'd ordered him!"

The Little Green Tractor looked up at the gigantic tractor in amazement.

"I'm Big Ben!" said the huge machine. "Thank you for putting me together. Will you be my best friend?"

"I'd like that," the Little Green Tractor sighed. "But I don't think the farmer will want me any more, now he has you!"

"Stuff and nonsense!" laughed the farmer. "I ordered Big Ben to help you." He patted the Little Green Tractor's bonnet. "I don't want to wear you out. I've got far too much land now for a little tractor like you."

So the Little Green Tractor was happy helping his friend Big Ben in the fields all day long.

And at night, they parked side by side in the farmer's new tractor shed.

Bathtime By The Sea

"I shan't be seeing you for a while," said Peter to his bathtime toys. "Tomorrow I am going on a week's holiday by the sea."

Then Peter dried each toy carefully on a towel, and put them back on the shelf by the side of the bath.

"That's dreadful news!" cried the toy sailor as soon as Peter had closed the bathroom door. "We shall miss seven nights of bathtime fun. It's just not fair!"

The poor bathroom toys spent a miserable night knowing that they would be left alone for a whole week.

Early next morning Peter rushed into the bathroom and scooped up his bathtime toys. He dropped them into the carrier bag, and his dad put them into the boot of his car with the rest of the luggage.

"It's a much better idea to take your toys from the bathroom on holiday," the whale and the penguin heard Peter's mum say. "Your teddy's fur would get soaking wet and full of sand, he's better left at home!"

"That means that we must be going to the seaside instead of teddy!" yelled the bathtime toys, and they hugged one another inside the carrier bag.

What a wonderful week it was. Peter took his toys down to the beach every single day.

He built a sand castle and dug a moat all the way round, then he filled the moat up with buckets of water from the sea.

Peter made the toy sailor 'King of the Castle', the penguin and the seal were guards, and the rest of the toys floated around in the moat - to save the castle from attack!

"What a great game this is!" laughed the whale. "I wish I could stay at the seaside for ever!"

That night the tide came in and washed Peter's sand castle away, but when the tide went out, it left behind rock pools full of all sorts of exciting creatures.

The rest of the holiday Peter played on the rocks while his bathtime toys explored the pools.

The seal and the whale raced and chased in and out with the rainbow-coloured fish, and the penguin made friends with a great big crab. The toy sailor went diving with the yellow ducks, and the sailing boats just bobbed up and down in the water.

"Time to go home!" said Peter at the end of the very last day.

So before they left the sea-shore the toys gathered a few of the prettiest shells to remind them of their first holiday by the sea.

Off To Camp

It was nearing the end of the long school summer holidays, and the little hedgehogs were feeling a bit bored.

"Can we go camping?" the eldest hedgehog asked his mother. And Mrs Hedgehog agreed, that if he would take charge, they could go.

So the ten little hedgehogs began to pack at once.

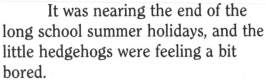

"We're going to camp! We're going to camp!" sang the youngest as he shoved his clothes and his books and his toys and all his bedding into a rucksack.

"I'll carry the tent!" one little hedgehog offered, but the tent was so heavy, it took four of them.

"We'll carry the pots and pans!" shouted two more.

So as soon as the ten little hedgehogs had packed everything they could possibly need, they set off to find a good place to camp.

They hadn't gone very far before Baby Hedgehog's legs felt very tired, and he asked to be carried.

A little further on, the two hedgehogs carrying the pots and pans tripped over, and everything went rolling down the lane.

"Let's try to put up a tent," said the eldest one who was in charge.

"Have any of you put up a tent before?" Baby Hedgehog asked, just out of interest - and nine little hedgehogs shook their heads.

They struggled and struggled all afternoon, the little hedgehogs were so busy, they had no time to stop for a meal - not even a tiny snack.

"I'm hungry," Baby Hedgehog cried. "It will be getting dark soon and I want to go home!"

Now the other little hedgehogs hadn't thought that they would be sleeping in a tent, in the dark, far away from their mum, and with no supper!

So quick as they could they packed up their things and raced for home.

Now when, at last, the ten little hedgehogs reached their garden gate it was almost dark.

"I smell fried bread," cried Baby Hedgehog. "And sausages and baked potatoes!"

"Welcome home," smiled their mother. "I thought I would camp in the garden tonight. Would you like to join me?"

And of course, they did!

Sylvester Winds The Clock

The Mayor was standing outside the town hall gazing up at the clock. He was looking very worried indeed.

"Whatever is the matter, Mr Mayor?" asked Sylvester the stork, as he strolled by with a few of his friends.

"It's the clock!" the Mayor replied, still looking up.

"Right on time!" said Sylvester looking carefully at his watch. "Four o'clock, on the dot!"

"The town hall clock is always exactly right," said the Mayor very grandly. "That isn't the problem."

"Then may I know what the problem is?" asked Sylvester the stork, polite as ever.

Suddenly the Mayor stared down at Sylvester's watch.

"Sylvester," said the Mayor with a smile. "I no longer have a problem, thanks to you!"...and Sylvester listened very carefully to what the Mayor had to say.

"I have to go away today," said the Mayor. "And I need a responsible stork with a watch, to wind the town hall clock."

Sylvester opened his beak to speak, but before he could utter one single word, the Mayor had handed over the clock key and vanished!

18

"How on earth am I going to get to the top of the clock tower?" cried Sylvester, very dismayed.

His friends opened their beaks to speak...

"Don't tell me!" cried Sylvester. "I need a ladder. No, I need two ladders, the clock tower is so high!"

Once again his friends opened their beaks to speak...but Sylvester had already found two ladders and was busy lashing them together with a rope.

"They're not long enough!" he wailed. "I need some scaffolding!"

Yet again his friends tried to say something...but Sylvester was in no mood to listen.

In a short while, a builder's truck drove up to the town hall carrying a load of scaffolding. Swiftly the pieces were bolted together and fitted all round the clock tower of the town hall.

"I can't climb up there!" cried poor Sylvester, and he hid his head under his wing...and his friends got a chance to speak at last...

"You silly stork!" they yelled all together. "The Mayor asked you to wind the clock, because he knew you could FLY up to the tower - and we've been trying to tell you all the time!"

19

Nina Puts Out The Fire

Nina's dad was a helicopter pilot. The little girl often saw him flying overhead, as she lived in a house quite near to the airfield.

Sometimes her dad would hover very low over their garden in his helicopter. Nina's dad also took her to the airfield to have a look round. There were lots of different planes on the ground, but Nina liked her dad's little helicopter best of all.

"Would you like to go up for a flight today?" her dad asked Nina.

"Yes please!" said Nina. "Can we fly over our garden and wave to Mum?"

So Nina and her dad climbed aboard and took off.

They hadn't gone very far before a call came through on the helicopter's radio.

"There's a huge grass fire on the side of the runway!" a voice said. "Our airfield fire-engine is being repaired. Can you help?"

Nina and her dad could see clouds of thick smoke rising from the airfield.

"If we don't do something quickly," said Nina's dad anxiously, "the grass fire will spread to the control tower!"

"Look down below," cried Nina.

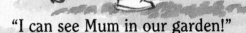

"I can see Mum in our garden!"

"We've no time to wave now!" yelled Nina's dad above the noise of the helicopter.

"Can you see my paddling pool?" shouted the little girl. "If we could hook it underneath the helicopter, and carry it across to the airfield, it might put out the fire!"

"Great idea!" nodded Nina's dad, and he hovered carefully over the garden, while Nina dropped ropes and hooks out of the helicopter door.

All the neighbours rushed outside to help and very soon the paddling pool was ready to go.

Nina's dad took his helicopter up high over the garden and flew very carefully across to the airfield.

"Let go of the ropes now!" he shouted to Nina as he hovered over the fire.

As the little girl let the ropes fall, all the water from the paddling pool dropped onto the flames.

The fire was put out at once and the control tower was safe...and Nina and her dad and the little helicopter, were given a great big cheer when they touched down!

Griselda In Charge

The farmer and his wife were planning to go away for the whole day. That meant the animals would be all alone.

"I'm rather worried about leaving Griselda," said the farmer. "Although she's a great favourite of mine, she can be such a scatterbrain and a really silly goose sometimes."

And as the farmer's wife looked across the farmyard, we could quite see what the farmer meant.

There was Griselda, flapping her wings, cackling and squawking as she raced round and round the farmyard.

"Whatever shall we do with that silly goose?" groaned the farmer shaking his head.

"I think I know the answer!" said the farmer's wife with a little secret smile.

Very early next morning before the farmer and his wife went away for the day they woke up Griselda and said. "You're in charge today!"...and off they went.

"What me? I can't believe it! It's not true!" Griselda gabbled, running round and round in panic.

Then all of a sudden she stopped, took a deep breath, then said quite calmly,

"I AM IN CHARGE!"

Without a moment's thought, Griselda flew up onto a pile of hay and began shouting orders to the astonished animals.

"Cows, march into the milking shed!

Pigs, hoe the turnips!

Sheep, rake the hay!

Donkey, take the milk to market!

Dog, drive the tractor!"

Griselda the goose wasn't finished yet, there were lots more orders to come.

"Goats, mend the barn roof!

Cats, tidy up the farmyard!

Turkey, pump the water!

And chickens, chop the firewood!"

When, at last, the farmer and his wife returned, they couldn't believe how much work had been done.

"What a sensible goose you've turned out to be!" said the farmer as he patted Griselda on the head.

"I just knew she would!" smiled the farmer's wife.

"It's very hard being in charge," cackled Griselda, flapping her wings and racing round and round the farmyard. "I'd much rather be silly!"

And the farmer and his wife just shook their heads and sighed...

23

Mr Fox Plays Statue

Have you ever played the statue game? - It's great fun!

...One person turns their back while everyone else runs about, and when that person turns around, everybody must keep perfectly still - just like a statue!

If you as much as blink, you are out! And the person who keeps still the longest is the winner.

What Mr Fox didn't know, was that Bobby Rabbit and his friends were hiding behind his garden shed. They were all holding empty baskets -

Bobby Rabbit and his friends loved playing statues, and one day they used their favourite game to trick crafty Mr Fox.

It happened in early summer.

Right in the middle of Mr Fox's garden was a big bed of ripe juicy strawberries.

"I shall keep watch day and night," said Mr Fox out loud, as he stood on guard in his garden. "Bobby Rabbit and his horrid little pals will never get my strawberries!"

just waiting to fill them with all those lovely ripe strawberries.

"Good afternoon, Mr Fox." called Bobby Rabbit. "I've never seen anyone stand so perfectly still! Can you play statues?"

"No-one is better at standing still than me," boasted Mr Fox. "And I'm brilliant at playing statues!"

"Would you show us how to play?" begged Bobby Rabbit trying hard not to giggle.

So Mr Fox left his strawberry patch, and went over to show Bobby Rabbit and his friends how to play the statue game.

"He's so good at it," sighed Bobby Rabbit, and he gazed at Mr Fox standing perfectly still.

As the game went on, the little animals crept away, one by one.

Quietly they sneaked into Mr Fox's strawberry patch, filled up their baskets then scurried off home.

At last the game came to an end, and Mr Fox was the only one left standing in the garden as still as a statue!

Now Bobby Rabbit should have told Mr Fox that he was the winner, but that crafty rabbit's mouth was too full of strawberries!

The Striped Submarine

The Striped Submarine always felt a bit sleepy in the afternoon, so most days she had a little nap and drifted drowsily just beneath the waves.

"I must have been asleep for hours," said the Striped Submarine. "It's got dark while I've been dreaming."

"No, it's not dark yet," laughed a passing jelly-fish. "A silly seagull has built her nest on top of your periscope!"

"Oh no!" gasped the Striped Submarine. "She'll have to find somewhere else, or I won't be able to dive down deep below the water!"

"I'm dreadfully sorry," cackled the silly seagull. "I've already laid three eggs, so I shall have to stay here until my chicks hatch and are big enough to fly away!"

"How long will that take?" asked the Striped Submarine, very shocked indeed.

"At least twelve weeks!" said the silly seagull.

The Striped Submarine heaved a great big sigh, and almost dived down to the bottom of the sea.

"Try to remember," the jelly-fish told the submarine, "you can go up but not down!"

So for twelve whole weeks, the Striped Submarine cruised round and round the ocean, with the silly seagull and her three chicks on top of her periscope.

As you can see, the ocean folks made quite sure she wasn't ever bored or lonely. And when the seagull chicks grew big and flew away - the Striped Submarine really missed them!

Belinda's Super-Duper Ice-Cream

It was the middle of the summer. The sun was blazing down from a clear blue sky making all the toys feel hot and tired. Even the toy soldier had changed into shorts and tee-shirt.

"Why don't you take your coat off?" the toy soldier asked Belinda the rag-doll.

"You know I hardly ever do that!" she snapped back, (really, Belinda was beginning to feel hot and tired too). "I shall have an ice-cream to keep cool!" Off she went to fetch one.

Now when Belinda returned, she was holding the biggest ice-cream you ever did see, but that selfish rag-doll couldn't be bothered to bring any ices back for the other toys.

"I shall eat my super-duper ice-cream in a moment" said Belinda taking a deep breath. "But first I shall tell you all about it!"...and she did.

"My super-duper ice-cream tastes of...strawberry and vanilla and fudge and toffee and butterscotch sauce with double chocolate chips and jelly beans on top!"

Sad to say, Belinda was so busy talking that her super-duper ice-cream melted away in the hot sun. It ran the whole way down her best coat and splashed onto her new shoes!

"Serves you right for being so selfish," laughed the toy soldier, and he rushed off to buy everyone an ice-cream.

As for Belinda - she spent the rest of that hot afternoon cleaning her best coat and new shoes!

Two Brave Little Astronauts

Two brave little astronauts went off to the Moon in a shiny silver rocket.

They both wore special space suits with lots of useful zips and pockets.

They had helmets on their heads and air-packs on their backs, and on their feet were absolutely enormous moon-boots.

As soon as they landed on the Moon, the two brave little astronauts walked all over the surface, and left very, very big footprints with their absolutely enormous moon-boots.

One of them whizzed off in the moon buggy while the other one gathered a bucketful of moon dust.

Then before they left for home one of them planted a flag to prove that the two brave little astronauts had really been to the moon.

"Time to go home!" said one to the other. So they headed back to Earth without delay.

At last they returned and splashed down safely in the sea.

One of the brave little astronauts opened the hatch to wave his flag and shout, "Hurrah!"

"Where did you get that flag?" asked the other.

"Some careless person left it on the Moon. I thought it made the place look untidy...so I brought it home!"

29

Emmy's Big Toe

Emmy the elephant hurt her big toe. She tripped over and banged it as she ran to get her breakfast.

"You great big silly!" cried Norah, the zoo-keeper's wife, as she served breakfast to the other animals.

"Ouch!" yelled Emmy, between mouthfuls of hot buttered toast. "Ouch, ouch, ouch!"

"Where does it hurt?" asked Norah kindly.

"My big toe!" Emmy yelled as she munched an extra slice.

"There, there!" said Norah. "We'd better let the vet take a look at you." And off she went to telephone him.

"Ouch!" yelled Emmy once again. The other animals felt sorry for her, so they made her lots more toast - just to make her feel better.

When the vet arrived to examine Emmy's big toe, he opened his black bag and took out a sticking plaster.

"Will it hurt?" Emmy gasped, still munching toast.

"Not a bit," the vet replied as he stuck on the plaster. "Rest that big toe for at least a week, young lady!" And off he went.

"Now that could be a bit of a problem," sighed Norah. "I don't think we have a wheel-chair big enough for you, Emmy!"

"I can't stay in the same place for a whole week!" wailed Emmy who by now had eaten every bit of the breakfast toast.

It wasn't long before the zoo-keeper came across to find out what had happened. He had heard Emmy shouting, "Ouch, ouch, ouch!" and wondered what was going on.

"She needs to rest her big toe!" said Norah. "Whatever are we going to do?"

"No problem at all!" cried the zoo-keeper, and off he went to telephone a factory nearby.

All the zoo animals stayed with Emmy to keep her company. Every so often she would shout, "Ouch, ouch, ouch!" Just to remind them that her big toe still hurt.

"It's arrived! It's arrived!" shouted the zoo-keeper as a lorry reversed carefully through the gates of the zoo.

There on the back, waiting to be unloaded...was a fork-lift truck!

"Perfect!" cried Norah quite delighted. "It's just the thing for taking Emmy round the zoo for a week!"

Norman The Nervous Ghost Train

Have you ever been on a Ghost Train? I have, and it's very scary.

This is the story of Norman the Nervous Ghost Train, who took children on a spooky ride at the fair.

Every day Norman carried passengers through long dark eerie tunnels, on a spine-chilling, nail-biting trip, where monsters spring out in front, skeletons rattle their bones all around, and big black hairy spiders dangle from the ceiling, and silky cobwebs brush your face, and make everyone scream and shriek!

"Isn't this fun!" cried one little boy who often went for a ride on the Nervous Ghost Train.

"Not one bit!" replied Norman shaking with fright. "I'll never get used to all those scary things inside that dark tunnel."

This made the little boy laugh out loud. "It's just pretend. The monsters aren't real. The ghosts are old white sheets and the spiders are bits of fur on string!"

"It's still very scary," mumbled the nervous Ghost Train feeling very embarrassed.

"You need a holiday with some fresh air and sunshine!" said the little boy. "Come with me to the country, and I promise you'll feel a lot better."

So the little boy drove the Nervous Ghost Train out of the fairground and never stopped until they reached the green fields and hills of the countryside.

As they sped along, they passed a field full of black and white cows.

"MOO! MOO! MOO!" they bellowed, and scattered in all directions.

It wasn't long before the Nervous Ghost Train gave a flock of sheep a terrible fright. They ran away as fast as they could, so did the rabbits and the pigs and all the fowls in the farmyard.

"Whatever is the matter with all the animals?" asked the nervous Ghost Train. "Who is making them so frightened?"

"You are!" smiled the little boy. "They've never seen a ghost train before."

"But they needn't be frightened of me," laughed Norman.

33

"And you shouldn't be frightened of those pretend monsters and skeletons and hairy spiders at the fairground!"

The Nervous Ghost Train looked down at the ground. "I have been a bit silly," he mumbled.

"I should say so!" said the little boy. "You must come to the countryside more often. The animals will soon get used to you."

"I could give them all a ride," suggested the Nervous Ghost Train - and he did!

After a while the little boy drove Norman back to the fairground, where a long queue of children stood waiting for a ride.

"Jump aboard," puffed the Nervous Ghost Train, "for the scariest ride of your lives!" This made the children shriek and scream at the tops of their voices!

"Watch out ghosts, skeletons and monsters, big hairy spiders and dangling cobwebs...HERE I COME!"

Then Norman the Nervous Ghost Train gave the little boy a great big wink, then disappeared into the long dark tunnel.

Don't Say Cuckoo!

When Mum read the children a bedtime story all the toys loved to listen.

"I do wish story-time could go on a bit longer," said one of the children.

"So do we!" whispered the toys very quietly.

"When the cuckoo clock on the wall says it's eight o'clock, I must close the storybook because it's bedtime," said Mum.

"Even if you haven't finished the story?" cried one of the children.

"I'm afraid so," said Mum quite firmly.

"One of us ought to have a word with that cuckoo clock," said the toy panda. "But I'm far too big and heavy to climb up there!"

So a few of the smaller and lighter toys decided to try.

At last they reached the cuckoo clock and knocked on the little door.

The cuckoo inside was delighted to meet them and said he would love to help. He agreed to keep quiet at eight o'clock (for a little while at least!).

"Your bedtime stories seem to take longer every night," said Mum as she carried on reading, but everyone was too busy listening to reply...especially the cuckoo in the clock on the wall!

Big Bear's New Bed

"I need a new bed!" said Big Bear one morning. "My head sticks out the top, and my toes out the bottom, and I'm afraid if I turn over during the night I shall fall out of bed onto the floor!"

And as Big Bear turned over, just to show the others what he meant, he rolled off the bed and landed on the floor with a thump.

This made the little bears laugh so much, they had to have several glasses of water to help them calm down!

"Why don't you leave it to us, Big Bear?" cried the little bears after breakfast. "We'll go and see the Bear Who Makes Furniture. He'll make a bed big enough for you!"

"How big is he?" asked the Bear Who Makes Furniture.

"He's as big as this!" said one little bear, stretching out his arms as wide as he could.

"He's much bigger than that!" argued the other little bears. "He's absolutely enormous!"

"He's at least as big as this!" cried three more of the little bears as they joined paws to form a circle.

"He must be a giant bear then!" gasped the Bear Who Makes Furniture.

At last the bed was finished. It took several of the strongest bears to carry it over to Big Bear's house.

"It's big enough for everyone!" joked Big Bear when he saw his brand new bed.

"Wonderful!" cried the little bears as they jumped up and down. "Now we can all share one great bed. Won't that be fun?"

...but Big Bear doesn't look too sure, does he?...

Mr Wolf's Big Sister

One day the three little pigs were strolling down the lane, when Mr Wolf came running by.

He didn't even notice the three little pigs, which was very strange, because he was always trying to catch them and gobble them up!

So the three little pigs followed Mr Wolf to find out what was going on.

At the bottom of the lane they spied him waiting at the bus stop.

"Perhaps Mr Wolf is going away, and he'll never bother us again!" said one little pig.

"No such luck!" moaned the other two.

Then along came the bus, and when it stopped Mr Wolf's big sister stepped off.

"She looks very fierce, just look at those teeth!" gasped the first little pig.

"She looks very strong, just look at those claws!" gasped the second little pig.

"She looks fine to me!" said the third little pig. "Shall I go over and say 'Hello'!"

"Indeed you will not!" the other two pigs cried. "Let's run home before they gobble up the lot of us!"

When they were safe inside the three little pigs sat down to think.

"Three little pigs like us are no match for Mr Wolf and his big sister," they agreed. "We'll have to think up a daring plan!"...and so they did.

The very next morning the three little pigs went over to Mr Wolf's house and knocked on his door.

One little pig was carrying a beautiful bunch of flowers. One had a big box of chocolates tied with a red ribbon, the other little pig was holding a huge basket of fruit.

"These gifts are for your beautiful big sister!" said the three little pigs grinning broadly (although their knees were knocking together loudly).

Now Mr Wolf was just about to grab hold of them, when his big sister stepped outside.

"For me?" she sighed, and she tickled each little pig on the nose.

Then she opened her chocolates and shared them with the three little pigs...and what is more...she made Mr Wolf do all the little pig's chores!

He mended the roof and painted the fence. He chopped enough firewood for a whole winter. He mowed the lawn and cut the hedge - he even swept the chimney!

"It's my way of saying 'Thank you' to these three sweet, kind and charming little pigs!" said Mr Wolf's big sister.

The New School

Minnie and Winnie had just moved house. They liked their new home. There was plenty of space and a big garden - so why did the girls look so glum?

Mrs Morris, their new neighbour, popped her head over the wall.

"Pleased to meet you, girls!" she called. "You both look as if you need cheering up."

"I do!" sighed Minnie, and she folded her arms.

"Me too!" agreed Winnie, and she did the same.

So Mrs Morris came into the garden to see what she could do.

"We start our new school tomorrow," said both girls together. "And we don't want to go. Not ever!"

Mrs Morris stepped back in amazement. "Is that the big school across the park, with playing fields all around?"

The twins nodded, still looking very glum.

"Is that the school that has hamsters and gerbils and fluffy baby rabbits, with a fish-pond and a bird-table in the garden?"

"We think so," said the girls looking interested.

"Is that the school where they bake cakes and go swimming, and have picnics in the summer and parties at Christmas time?"

"We hope so, Mrs Morris!" and the twins ran inside to get ready for school in the morning.

Next day Minnie and Winnie could not wait to get to school.

As they opened their classroom door, they heard a familiar voice say, "Welcome Minnie and Winnie. I'm your new teacher, Mrs Morris!"

Don't Open The Box

Helen the hamster was very inquisitive. She often poked her little pink nose where it wasn't wanted.

"I'm just curious!" said Helen as she tried all the perfumes and powders on someone else's dressing table.

"Do try not to be so nosey!" complained one of Helen's friends as the little hamster peered into all her kitchen cupboards.

Now one day, Helen the hamster found a mysterious wooden box on the floor.

"I must find out what's inside!" said Helen as she tried to lift the lid.

"It's locked!"she cried, and that made the little hamster more curious than ever.

"I'm sure I can guess where the key is!"Of course inquisitive Helen found it straight away.

"Someone doesn't want me to know what's inside the box!" sniggered Helen, and she turned the key.

As she did, a strange whirring sound seemed to come from inside the box.

"It's a music box," Helen smiled. "I knew it all the time!"

Then, without any warning, the lid of the box flew open...and out popped a Jack-in-the-Box!

He gave poor Helen the fright of her life.

"Serves you right!" he cackled. "That's what you get for being nosey!".

41

The Haunted Glade

Messenger Mole delivered the mail all around the wood. His aunt, Miss Mole, sorted out the letters for every animal that lived in the woodland.

"How very odd," remarked Miss Mole, one day, "They're all the same!"

It took Messenger Mole all morning to deliver the letters, and by lunchtime he was quite exhausted.

His last call was at the house of Mr Grey Badger.

"Let's open our letters together," suggested Messenger Mole to the badger. "Mine's an invitation to a party at midnight in the Haunted Glade deep in the wood!"

"So is mine," said Mr Grey Badger waving his letter in the air. "It looks very suspicious to me!"

"Nonsense!" cried Messenger Mole. "I'm going!" And off he scuttled.

All that day the animals showed one another their party invitations - they were all the same!

"I don't like going anywhere near the Haunted Glade," whispered Miss Mole, "It's so dark and spooky!"

"Nonsense!" said Messenger Mole. "We'll all go together and carry lanterns. It would be a shame to miss a party."

"Sounds like fun to me," squeaked Mildred Mouse.

So the woodland animals busied about all the rest of that day, looking for their party clothes and ironing out the creases wherever necessary.

Only Mr Grey Badger decided to stay at home. "Don't know what all the fuss is about," he muttered to anyone who would listen. "I think it's very suspicious inviting us all to visit the Haunted Glade at midnight." A strange look came over his face. "I shall go indoors and do some thinking!"

Once it grew dark, the animals changed into their party clothes and waited.

"It seems an awfully long time to midnight," said Mildred Mouse, who was having a hard time keeping her little ones awake.

Mrs Grey Rabbit, on the other hand, had put all her bunnies to bed at six o'clock, and promised she would wake them at eleven, in time to get

ready and reach the Haunted Glade by midnight.

At last it was almost time. Small groups of animals carrying torches and lamps gathered outside their front doors.

"Are you sure you won't join us and come to the party?" asked Messenger Mole as he passed Mr Grey Badger's house.

"No!" replied Badger, who was dressed up in a dark hat and overcoat and carrying his cricket bat. "I've got work to do!"

"At midnight?" thought Messenger Mole who quickly forgot all about Badger and joined Mildred Mouse and several others who were heading for the Haunted Glade.

It was a very long walk in the dark and cold.

"Is the Haunted Glade really haunted?" asked one little rabbit.

"Listen!" whispered a fox cub. "I think I can hear ghosts moaning and groaning!" This made all the young animals shake with fright.

"Stop being so silly!" snapped Mrs Grey Rabbit. "We've been invited to a party, so let's get a move on, it's almost twelve o'clock."

"Ghosts come out on the stroke of midnight!" said a little rabbit in a trembling voice.

"Now that's just silly!" his mother replied.

At long last they reached the Haunted Glade...and what do you think they found...NOTHING...no lights, no party food or balloons and no music for dancing - in fact the Haunted Glade was completely empty.

"I think we've been tricked," said Mrs Grey Rabbit. "There's no party at all!"

Slowly the animals trudged back to their homes in the familiar part of the wood... And there was Mr Grey Badger waiting to welcome them home.

"We've all been tricked!" said Messenger Mole quietly.

"You certainly have!" Mr Badger replied, as a broad grin spread across his face, which made the animals feel even more embarrassed.

"I thought there was something very odd about those invitations," said Badger beginning to enjoy himself. "So I stayed here to see what would happen, and my suspicions were quite correct."

"Do tell us what happened!" begged Messenger Mole as he tugged at Badger's overcoat.

"This is what happened!"and he switched on a powerful light outside his front door.

There, in a heap on the ground, were two wicked stoats and an evil weasel. They were tied up with ropes and gagged with several of Miss Mole's best scarves, and scattered all around were some of the woodland creatures' most treasured possessions.

"You've been burgled!" announced Badger, grabbing one of the stoats by the scruff of the neck and holding him up high.

Everyone gasped!

"While you were away at this so-called party, these three no-good fellows broke into your houses and stole everything," went on Mr Badger.

"Then those party invitations I delivered were nothing but a trick!" cried poor Messenger Mole.

"Absolutely!" said Badger. "It's lucky I stayed behind!"

"Very lucky!" cried Mildred Mouse and Mrs Grey Rabbit, and they rushed forward to give Badger a hug and a kiss.

"Steady on!" said Badger blushing. "Now off to bed everyone. You must all be very tired - especially the little ones. I shall lock these three fellows in my cellar and deal with them in the morning."

So the tired woodland animals picked up all their treasures that had been stolen and stumbled off to bed.

"It's a good job we've got a clever chap like you to look after us, Badger," said Messenger Mole as he rubbed his eyes.

"It certainly is!" agreed Mr Badger as he handed the mole a cup of strong tea.

"Tomorrow afternoon, at three o'clock sharp, I shall give a party. There'll be fancy cakes and salad sandwiches, and we'll have games with prizes and music for dancing!" announced Badger as he poured himself some more tea.

"Messenger Mole! Will you take out the invitations first thing in the morning?"...but Messenger Mole was already fast asleep.

Balloons Everywhere

Lewis went to a wedding. At the party afterwards there were lots and lots of lovely balloons.

They were tied to all the tables and chairs with bright shiny ribbons...big balloons, little balloons, and very special balloons that scattered pretty confetti all over the room when they went POP!

Lewis and the rest of the children at the wedding had a wonderful time with so many balloons to play with.

They raced and chased round and round until they were tired out.

Then one by one they sat down with a FLOP, and let go of their balloons... What do you think happened?...

...One by one the balloons floated up to the ceiling and stayed there.

The children were most upset - except one!

Lewis had noticed the balloons fixed to the tables and chairs. So when he wanted to jump about and have fun, he tied his balloons to his wrist and some round his middle.

Clever boy, Lewis! But be careful you don't float up to the ceiling and stay there!

Vera Takes A Shower

Vera the viper was very vain. She simply could not stop admiring herself.

"I look so pretty," Vera said as she passed a puddle. "No, I'm wrong!" sighed the vain viper as she gazed at her own reflection, "I look absolutely beautiful!"

Now the garden was very damp that morning, so Vera spent lots of time admiring herself as she went from puddle to puddle.

Then all at once, as she slithered along, Vera came across another snake.

"How plain she looks!" hissed Vera rudely. "How skinny and how boring!"

Then without any warning, a shower of icy water hit Vera in the face.

"What a nasty-tempered snake!" gasped poor Vera, soaking wet and very cold.

Little did Vera know, she had been talking to the GARDEN HOSE.

Emilio's Present

It was Emilio's birthday. The little Mexican boy had been given lots of presents and he felt very happy.

"There is one more very special gift," said Emilio's father. "But first you must promise that you will look after it always."

So Emilio promised, then ran off to find his very special birthday present.

As Emilio ran round the side of the house he could hardly believe his eyes. For there, standing in the middle of the yard, was his very own little donkey.

"I shall call you Paco!" said Emilio as he led his new friend across the yard for a cool drink.

Now Paco was far too small to reach the water trough, but the little Mexican boy soon solved the problem.

"I promised to look after you always," laughed Emilio. "And I will!"

49

Nipper's New Wheels

One dreadful day, Nipper the pull-along dog lost his wheels! One by one they fell off and vanished without trace in the garden.

"Poor Nipper!" said the toy robot. "What are you going to do?"

"Not a lot!" replied Nipper sadly. "Without my wheels, I could stay in the same place for ever!"

"Let's take a good look round," suggested the red-haired clown. "We might find something that's the same shape as your lost wheels."

So the toys began to search at once.

It wasn't long before one of them discovered a bag of big chocolate coins that belonged to the children.

"They're just perfect!" cried the red-haired clown, and with a bit of help he fixed them onto Nipper.

The chocolate wheels worked quite well for a while, until the front ones melted when the sun shone through the window, and the pet gerbil nibbled the back ones.

"Perhaps we could find some spare wheels at the bottom of the old toy chest," said the robot. "It's full of bits and pieces!"

So with a bit of effort, the toys tipped up the chest and began to search at once.

"Look what I've found!" cried one of the toys, holding up a forgotten treasure.

"I didn't know this was in here," shouted another.

"I've never seen so much rubbish," poor Nipper sighed as he gazed at all the different spare wheels...

...There were bike wheels, pram wheels, all sorts of steering wheels, gear wheels and car wheels and every different size of wheel...but not one of the wheels would fit Nipper the pull-along dog.

"Look here!" cried a delighted doll. "I've found my old necklace and my red belt. I thought they'd gone for ever!" So she put them on straight away.

"Here's my key!" said the clockwork ladybird. "Will someone wind me up?"

"I've found the trophy I won last year!" yelled the model racing driver.

"And here's the sheep-dog from the toy farm!" smiled Angie the peg-doll.

"Everybody's found something they've liked or lost," said Nipper looking very disappointed. "But I can't seem to find any wheels that will fit me!"

Then suddenly, out of the old toy chest, rolled a bright yellow roller-skate.

"I'm the only one left of the pair," said the skate as he introduced himself to Nipper. "I'm no good on my own, but my wheels are just right for you!"

So the toys lifted Nipper on top of the skate, and he fitted perfectly.

"I'm even better than before!" laughed Nipper as he whizzed round the floor.

"It's my super-fast wheels!" cried the roller-skate happily... he'd been left alone and forgotten for far too long!

51

Ziggie Wanders Off

All day long, Ziggie the little zebra munched sweet green grass on the big open plains of Africa.

Now Ziggie, as a rule, did as he was told and stayed close by his mother.

But one very hot afternoon, Ziggie felt so thirsty, he wandered off all by himself in search of a drink.

In a short while he came to a lake, and as he bent down and opened his mouth for a drink, another little zebra did too!

Ziggie tossed his head, and so did the other little zebra.

Ziggie wiggled his ears, and the other little zebra did the same.

"Stop copying me!" shouted Ziggie, but the other little zebra just stared back.

Then came a lot of giggling and laughing, and all the young animals standing around were very amused..

"Your new zebra friend can't speak back," giggled a baby hippo.

"You've been talking to your own reflection, Ziggie!" The little animals burst out laughing once more.

"Don't worry!" smiled a young giraffe. "We've all made the same mistake. Lots of us come to drink at this lake twice a day, so you need never be short of new friends!"

Dad Phones Home

Dolly, Polly and Molly were always talking on the telephone. They rang their friends and their friends rang them back and they chattered for hours and hours.

The three girls made phone calls about swimming arrangements and dancing lessons and parties.

They rang the cinema and the theatre, the railway station and the store.

They talked to the doctor, the dentist, the vet and the hairdresser... poor Dad was never able to use the phone at all!

Then one day, Dolly, Polly and Molly looked out of the window, and there was Dad making a phone call from his very own phone box ... in the garden!

Snarl Please!

Tiny Tiger Tim thought that he would take his new camera into the jungle with him.

"I shall take photographs of all the fierce and dangerous animals that live there!" he said. "When I find any of them snarling or snapping or grinding their teeth - I shall take a photo at once!"

So Tiny Tiger Tim put a film in his camera, popped his shady hat on his head and set off.

He hadn't gone very far into the steaming hot jungle when he met a leopard... all teeth and claws!

"Snarl please," said Tiny Tiger Tim as he pointed at his camera.

"So sorry," said the leopard. "I'm busy taking a shower - got to smell fresh, goodbye!"

Next Tiny Tiger Tim came upon an orang-utan sitting in the trees... he was an ugly fellow!

"Look nasty for the camera," said Tiny Tiger Tim.

"No time today," the orang-utan smiled. "I have to practise my flute - I have an exam tomorrow!"

So Tiny Tiger Tim went on his way. Suddenly he spied a boa-constrictor hanging from a branch.

"Hiss if you please," said Tiny Tiger Tim as he pointed his camera.

"Not a chance!" replied the snake as he grasped his feather duster

tightly. "I'm busy cleaning my bedroom. Please go away, unless you like dusting!"

So Tiny Tiger Tim walked on through the undergrowth until he came to a crocodile.

"Give us a grin and show us those razor-sharp teeth!" Tiny Tiger Tim joked as he focused his lens.

"I'm just about to eat this plateful of marmalade sandwiches," smiled the crocodile. "You can join me if you wish."... But Tiny Tiger Tim

moved on... the crocodile looked far too ordinary with a big white napkin tucked under his chin!

All of a sudden a parrot squawked loudly overhead. Crashing through the undergrowth came one of the most fierce and bad-tempered creatures of the jungle - a huge two horned rhinoceros.

Straight away Tiny Tiger Tim was ready with his camera.

"How lovely to see you!" giggled the rhino with delight. "I need a little help with my lines for

tomorrow night's show. It's called Jungle Jingles, and I'm the funny comedian!"

"I don't believe it," cried Tiny Tiger Tim as he glanced around.

"Jungle animals are supposed to be fierce and frightening!" yelled Tiny Tiger Tim at the top of his voice. Then he put down his camera and he roared and roared and roared!

He made so much noise that everyone from miles around came to take photographs of THE FIERCEST TIGER IN THE JUNGLE!

The Fat Ginger Cat

"I wish we could do something about that Fat Ginger Cat!" whispered the mice as Ginger stuck his head through the cat-flap.

Quickly the mice ran away into the bushes before they were caught.

"He's everywhere!" complained a brown mouse.

"We can't get into the kitchen to eat up the cake crumbs and cheesy biscuits," said another.

"It's as bad in the garden," sobbed a pretty little mouse with a pink bow. "We should be eating picnic food and tasty treats from the barbecue, but that Fat Ginger Cat gobbles up everything in sight!"

"He'll gobble you up too," called a Robin as he flew by. "Be careful! Be careful!"

"The robin is right," said the brown mouse. "Something must be done about that Fat Ginger Cat!"

Just at that moment, a dark shadow passed overhead.

"Nothing to worry about," called the brown mouse to everyone. "It's only a hot-air balloon!"

In the next few minutes giant balloons of all shapes and sizes floated across the sky.

"Aren't they beautiful?" sighed the pretty little mouse with the pink bow.

"They certainly are," agreed the brown mouse. "Now, these hot-air balloons have given me a brilliant idea!"

The Fat Ginger Cat never noticed the giant Balloons as they drifted by, he was fast asleep snoring in the warm sun.

"I need six of the strongest mice straight away!" announced the brown mouse, looking very serious. "We are going to buy a balloon!"

After what seemed a very long time, the six strong mice came back with a large parcel and a huge ball of string.

The brown mouse unwrapped the parcel.

"Start pumping!" he cried, and the six strong mice did just that.

"Whatever is it?" asked the pretty little mouse with the pink bow.

"It's a very special Balloon that will scare the wits out of that Fat Ginger Cat!" the brown mouse sniggered.

"It's a GIANT MOUSE!" squeaked the pretty little mouse with the pink bow. "And it's even bigger than that Fat Ginger Cat!"

As the giant mouse slowly rose into the air, the Fat Ginger Cat, who was still asleep in the sun, lazily opened one eye.

The great balloon gave him such a fright, he jumped up with all four paws in the air.

"I'll never chase mice again as long as I live!" screeched the Fat Ginger Cat, and he dived into the bushes.

How the mice cheered and cheered, they were safe at last from that Fat Ginger Cat.

57

Elvis And The White Bear Cubs

Elvis the Eskimo heard a strange scratching and snuffling noise. It seemed to be coming from outside his igloo.

"It must be visitors," said Elvis, "and they can't find my doorbell!"

So straight away he put on his warm clothes and stepped outside to see who it could be.

"We're lost!" said a couple of tiny voices. Two polar bear cubs were huddled together behind the igloo.

"I'm not surprised," joked Elvis. "I can hardly see you myself in the white snow!"

Just at that moment Mother Bear came lumbering across the ice.

"I can never find these two!" she grumbled. "As soon as I let them go out to play, they vanish into thin air!"

"I can quite believe that," agreed Elvis as the huge polar bear towered above him.

Now the two little bear cubs were as white as the snow around them, but Elvis knew exactly how to solve their mother's problem.

He went inside his igloo and very soon came out with two brightly coloured track-suits.

"I wore these when I was small, and my mum could always find me!"

Straight away the two little bear cubs pulled on their new clothes.

"Let's play hide and seek!" they yelled as they ran off into the snow.

"I don't think so!" chuckled Mother Bear and Elvis the Eskimo.

Quack, Quack, Mr Fox

Bobby Rabbit was looking in a drawer one day when he came across a strange kind of whistle.

He took a deep breath and blew down the hole in the top with all his might.

"Quack, quack!" came the sound. "Quack, quack!"

"It's not a whistle at all!" laughed Bobby Rabbit. "It's a duck-call!" And he blew hard again. "Quack, quack! Quack, quack!"

"I could have some fun with this," Bobby Rabbit giggled, and he ran down the road to Mr Fox's house, and hid behind the hedge.

Now when Bobby Rabbit saw Mr Fox open his back door, he took out the duck-call and blew as hard as he could.

"Quack, quack! Quack, quack!"

"Do I hear a duck?" asked Mr Fox listening very hard. "Yes I do! Yes I do!" And he jumped up and down in excitement.

Straightaway Mr Fox rushed indoors. He lit his stove and put a huge pan of water to boil on the top.

"I shall have tasty roast duck with green beans and carrots for dinner tonight!" he sang at the top of his voice.

Now Bobby Rabbit, who was still hiding behind the hedge, laughed so much he could hardly blow down the duck-call.

Suddenly Mr Fox rushed out of his house. "I can't hear the duck," he gasped, looking very worried. "I hope it hasn't flown away!"

So Bobby Rabbit stopped giggling and blew on the duck-call at once.

"Quack, quack! Quack, quack!"

"Splendid, splendid!" cried Mr Fox. "Duck for my dinner. What a treat!"

While he was outside listening to the duck quacking, Mr Fox picked up a bunch of carrots and a basket of green beans from his vegetable plot.

"My favourites!" whispered Bobby Rabbit from behind the hedge.

"Quack, quack! Quack, quack!"

At last the time came for Mr Fox to go behind the hedge and catch the duck for his dinner.

What a shock he got when he found Bobby Rabbit sitting there, blowing his duck-call.

"Quack, quack! Quack, quack!"

Mr Fox was so angry that he threw down his basket of vegetables and had a temper-tantrum on the spot!

Quick as a flash, Bobby Rabbit grabbed the vegetables and ran for his life.

"Green beans and fresh carrots - my favourites!" he yelled as he ran home.

"Quack, quack! Quack, quack!"

61

The Rabbit's Bedtime Story

It was getting late and almost time for the little grey rabbits to go to bed.

"Just time for a short story before I say goodnight," said their mother. So she sat down in her chair, picked up a storybook and reached inside her bag for her glasses.

"Oh dear!" said Mrs Grey Rabbit. "My bag is so full of all sorts of things, my glasses must have slipped right down to the bottom!"

First, she pulled out a packet of candy-canes, one for each of her little rabbits to nibble.

Next she found six odd socks then a golf club and a beach ball.

"I seem to have collected an awful lot of rubbish!" laughed Mrs Grey Rabbit as she pulled a mouth-organ from her bag, and an old fishing-net and a seaside spade.

By now Mrs Grey Rabbit had almost reached the bottom of her bag.

"No sign of my glasses, I'm afraid!" and she pulled out the very last object - an alarm clock that began to ring very loudly.

"Oh my goodness!" gasped Mrs Grey Rabbit. "It's eight o'clock. Time all of you were in bed!"

"But we haven't had our bedtime story yet!" cried the little grey rabbits all at once.

"And I still haven't found my glasses!" said their mother shaking her head.

So the little grey rabbits began searching the room as fast as they could...in cupboards and drawers, under tables and on top of cupboards, behind the curtains and up the chimney. They even looked under the floorboards!

All of a sudden the youngest rabbit leapt into the air. "I've found them! I've found them!" he cried, and in his paw were Mother Rabbit's lost glasses.

"They were down the side of her chair all the time!" shrieked the baby rabbit.

"Gather round quickly," said Mrs Grey Rabbit popping her glasses on the end of her nose. "We've just got time for one short-story...

Once upon a time there lived a beautiful young girl and her name was Cinderella. One night she went to a ball in a great palace and she lost her glass slipper..."

Every one of the little rabbits listened quietly right to the very end of the story - except baby rabbit, who had fallen asleep at the beginning!

Wake Up Lucille

Lucille the lop-eared rabbit was always late.

She was late getting up in the morning, she was late for lunch - and at the end of the day, when bedtime came - she was late for that too!

"Tomorrow we are going on holiday together," one of her friends told Lucille that night as she got ready for bed.

"My case is packed, I've cleaned my shoes, and my clothes are all ready for tomorrow," said Lucille as she busied about checking all her clocks and watches.

"Up at six o'clock sharp!" she muttered as she set her alarm clock. "I won't be late! I won't be late!"

Now as you may have noticed, Lucille's ears are very long. So most of the time she never hears her alarm clock ring - although it makes a very loud noise.

"How can I make really sure that I'll get up at six o'clock in the morning?" said the rabbit as she gazed around the room.

"I've got it!" shouted Lucille. "I'll sleep in the grandfather clock, then I'll be sure to hear the clock strike six, and I won't be late for my holiday!"

Peter's Present

Peter was looking for a present. "It's my brother's birthday tomorrow," he told the lady in the shop, "so I must find a present today!"

"How about some brown socks?" asked the lady.

"Too boring!" replied Peter.

"A white cotton shirt?" She held one up.

"Too plain!" Peter said, shaking his head.

"A box of handkerchiefs?" suggested the lady.

"Far too dull!" said Peter, and he thanked her and walked away.

Now as Peter strolled through the store wondering what to buy, he passed by the kitchen department. All around him he saw frying pans and kettles and big glass storage jars full of pasta.

"He won't want any of those," and Peter gave a little sigh.

Then, suddenly, behind the egg-whisks and the soup ladles, Peter caught sight of something his brother would really like. So he took out his money and bought the present.

Next morning Peter's brother was delighted when he unwrapped his gift.

"These are just perfect for me!" he said with a grin.

You see, Peter's brother was a circus clown, and he had broken all his breakfast pots practising his tricks.

"My old cups and saucers were very plain and boring," laughed Peter's brother. "These are just what I need and I promise not to break them!"

"Come on," said Peter. "Let's have some breakfast!"

The Wasp That Flew Round The World

Wilf the wasp went on a journey. It wasn't a very long journey, although he flew round the world.

The other insects were really impressed.

"Our very own Wilf the Wasp has flown right round the world all by himself!" they buzzed. "How did you do it in such a short time?"

"Follow me!" cried Wilf. "And I'll show you!"

First Wilf flew over the lawn, twice round the rose bushes, in through the open window of Honeysuckle Cottage... ROUND THE WORLD... and out through the window!

"You tricked us!" mumbled the bumble-bee.

"So I did," hummed Wilf. "And now I'm going round the world again - but this time I shall land on Japan or Australia, or possibly Spain!" And off he went!

Monty The Mountie

One day Monty the Mountie got a very important phone call.

"As you are such a marvellous mountie," said the Chief of all the Mounties, on the other end of the line, "I am sending you to the Great Whispering Pine Forest to keep a sharp look-out for desperate criminals. I know you are the right man for the job," the Chief of the Mounties went on, "so good luck marvellous Monty Mountie!" And he rang off.

So Monty the Mountie packed his spare uniform and a map, and set off to find the Great Whispering Pine Forest.

Monty drove all day, and just before the sun set behind the mountain, he came upon a log cabin-his new post. Outside was a tall flagpole with the Mountie's special flag flying from the top.

"Here at last!" said Monty the Mountie, as he saluted smartly. "I'd better get unpacked and settled in before nightfall!"

Now Monty's log cabin was rather small, but it was warm and comfortable and had everything a Mountie needed.

"Tomorrow," yawned Monty, who was feeling very tired, "I shall begin my search for desperate criminals. But tonight I shall cook myself some pancakes with maple syrup, then go straight to bed!"

So Monty set the table, popped a pile of fresh pancakes onto the warm plate and was just about to pour on the maple syrup, when there came a knock at the door.

"Do I smell maple syrup on warm pancakes?" a small voice asked.

And when Monty the Mountie opened the cabin door, he found a tiny chipmunk standing there.

"It's getting rather dark and cold outside," said the little fellow. "Can I come inside and have some supper?"

"Certainly!" smiled Monty, who was feeling a bit lonely. "I've made enough pancakes to feed the whole of the Great Whispering Pine Forest!"

"In that case," giggled the little chipmunk, "can my friend the rabbit and his friends the raccoons come in too?"

"Plenty of room and plenty of pancakes!" laughed Monty, and he opened the cabin door wide.

"How about me?" shouted a big brown bear as he lumbered out of the trees.

"Leave room for us!" called a couple of squirrels, and they scampered across the clearing and hurried into the cabin.

When at last Monty closed the door, he gazed across his cabin in surprise.

It was packed full of animals from the forest. Some were eating pancakes, others were drinking mugs of hot coffee, and one or two of the smaller animals had fallen asleep in front of the fire.

"Are you all staying the night?" asked Monty as he looked round and saw several beavers he hadn't noticed before.

"Yes please!" everyone replied, and begun getting ready for bed at once.

All of a sudden Monty the Mountie felt somebody tugging at his sleeve.

"Nobody wants to sleep near me!" It was a small skunk who had brought his own sleeping bag.

"How did you get in here?" gasped Monty, who by now couldn't find a place to sleep at all.

The little skunk looked very glum.

"I'll tell you what!" said Monty. "We'll both sleep outside tonight. I'll light a camp-fire and we'll both be warm and cosy."

And so he did!

"Well, I'm certainly not going to be lonely in my new home," Monty sighed as he looked up at the night sky. "Although my new friends are not going to fit into my log cabin for long. Tomorrow I shall have to find them somewhere else to live!"

But that's another story...

69

Pass The Parcel

The lifeboat crew had nothing to do one day. The weather was fine - no wind or rain, and the sea was calm and still.

"Everybody is being very sensible today," said one of the crew. "No-one has dropped off to sleep on their air-bed and floated out to sea, and nobody has been cut off by the tide or been stranded on the rocks!"

Just then the postman arrived at the lifeboat station. "No letters today lads!" cried the postman cheerfully, and all the lifeboat men groaned.

"But there is a parcel, and it's addressed to all of you!" And the postman went on his way.

"I wonder what it is?" asked a lifeboat man. "Let's open it and see!"

"Wait a minute!" said the coxswain of the lifeboat. "As we have nothing else to do at the moment... Let's play Pass the Parcel."

All the lifeboat men cheered loudly.

"I haven't played Pass the Parcel since I was a little boy!" said one.

"Neither have I!" chuckled another. "But I can remember how to play - First everyone sits in a big circle, and when the music plays the parcel is passed round and whoever is holding the parcel when the music stops - starts to unwrap it."

"I'll be in charge of the music." said the coxswain. "Come on lads, let's begin!"

Quickly the lifeboat men passed the parcel around, and one by one they tore off the wrapping paper.

"This parcel's getting smaller and smaller," said one of the crew. "Soon there'll be nothing left!"

"I think this must be the last layer!" shouted one of the men as the parcel was tossed to him.

"Hurry up!" yelled the man next to him. "Pull the string and find out what's inside!"

...And find out what they did!

As the lifeboat man pulled hard on the string, there was a noise like air coming from a balloon... and suddenly, in the middle of the circle, was a huge inflatable life-raft - growing bigger every second!

It gave the crew such a shock, that several of them fell over backwards.

"Come on, lads!" yelled the coxswain, switching off the music. "No time for games, let's go down to the shore and launch our new life-raft!"

71

Madeleine Brings The House Down

When Pierre played his accordion and whistled a tune, people loved to dance to the music.

Sometimes Pierre's wife Madeleine would sing along - now that was a different story!

Madeleine's voice was so high and shrill, that when she hit a top note, the noise would shatter glass!

She had broken all the windows in her house and cracked her best mirror too!

"I think your singing is simply beautiful," sighed Pierre as he played Madeleine's favourite tune on his accordion.

The more Madeleine sang, the more damage she caused. Houses began to shake, and chimney pots fell off buildings. Even the church spire began to look crooked when Madeleine sang nearby.

One day a gentleman asked Pierre if he would come and play his accordion in the street near his house.

Pierre agreed, and Madeleine came along to sing a song or two.

Halfway through the second verse of Madeleine's favourite french folksong, the gentleman began to beam with pleasure.

"It must be your beautiful voice," Pierre smiled at Madeleine. "Sing louder, dear!"

All of a sudden there was an almighty crash and the gentleman's house fell down!

"Thank you so much, Madeleine!" cried the gentleman as he kissed her hand. "My old house needed pulling down so I can build a new one - and you have demolished it for me with your incredible singing!"

Rosalind Learns To Read

The whole family was very proud when Rosalind learned to read. Grandma and Granddad ordered her a whole set of encyclopedias with lots of reading and hardly any pictures.

Mum and Dad went to the bookshop and bought Rosalind a whole pile of books about ponies and princesses and adventures on magic islands.

Rosalind read them all!

One afternoon when everybody was sitting together, Rosalind took out one of her books and opened it at the first page.

"Shall I read you all the story of the Princess and the Pea?" the little girl asked, and everyone agreed that they would love to listen.

"Once upon a time..." Rosalind began - and she carried on until she had read the whole story.

"Would you like to hear another one?" asked Rosalind. So she picked up another storybook and began again.

Rosalind read another story, then another and another... and every one listened spellbound...or so Rosalind thought!

Dickie's Dragon

"There's a dragon in the garden!" said Dickie to his mother one day.

"How very nice, dear," murmured his mother, who was making a sponge cake at the time. "What does he look like?"

"He's scaly and green with a forked tail. His nostrils are enormous and he can breathe fire... but most of the time he just puffs out smoke!" replied Dickie, who always described things perfectly.

"How very nice, dear," said his mother as she watched her sponge cake slowly sink in the middle.

So Dickie went out to tell his dad.

"There's a dragon in the garden!" said Dickie.

"Has he got big feet?" asked his dad.

"Gigantic!" Dickie replied. "They're flat with three giant toes and long hooked toe-nails!"

"Then tell him to keep off my seeds!" said dad, without even noticing he was raking over the ground where the dragon had left his footprints.

"What did you say was in the garden?" asked dad.

"A dragon!" Dickie replied.

"Show me!" said Dad.

"He's gone now," said Dickie, "but you can see where he's been!"

75

Little Silver Stream's Secret

Little Silver Stream had a secret. He had been busy for a whole week.

Early in the morning, he would creep quietly past the Wig-Wams where everybody was still fast asleep inside. Then he would run swiftly until he came to a bend in the river, where the mud was soft and sticky - just perfect for making pots.

Now Little Silver Stream had broken most of his mother's best pots - quite by accident, of course! So for a whole week he had been making new pots for her and drying them in the hot sun.

At last they were ready, and Little Silver Stream carried them carefully back to his village.

Now everybody wanted to know what Little Silver Stream had been up to, so they gathered round to take a look.

Sad to say, as soon as Little Silver Stream placed his pots on the table - they fell over,...and you can see why!

Little Silver Stream had forgotten to make the bottoms of his pots flat!

The whole village laughed at Little Silver Stream, and the little boy hung his head in shame.

"What good is a pot that doesn't hold water!" someone shouted. "We should name you Little Silly Stream instead!"

Now Little Silver Stream's mother was very wise. Straightaway she went to the river and made several rings of clay. She left them to bake in the hot sun and went back for them the next day.

When she came home she placed each pot on top of a clay ring. They fitted perfectly and the pots didn't fall over.

Little Silver Stream and his mother filled their new pots right up to the brim with water.

"I love my new pots," laughed Little Silver Stream's mother, "because you made them especially for me!"

77

The Playboat

Fisherman Bill was fishing in the sea one day when his boat sprang a leak.

"Goodness me!" cried Fisherman Bill when he saw the size of the hole at the bottom of his boat. "If I don't get a move on, I shall sink!"

So Fisherman Bill rowed like mad, and reached the shore just in time.

"You're getting far too old to go out to sea fishing," said Fisherman Bill's wife as she helped him pull the leaking boat up onto the beach.

"You're quite right, my dear," Fisherman Bill agreed. "From now on I shall fish with my rod and line from the pier."

As Fisherman Bill's wife gazed at the old boat, she had an idea.

"I shall fill your old boat with pretty plants and flowers," she said with a smile. "It will look lovely in front of our cottage."

Fisherman Bill began to look rather worried because he knew he would have to water those plants at least twice a day - and he hated gardening!

"I have a much better idea," he said crossing his fingers, "I'll fill my old boat with sand, then all the children can bring their toys and play inside it!"

What a good idea!

Iggy Babysits

Iggy promised that he would look after all the baby frogs while the older ones went to a party.

"It won't be easy!" said Silver Minnow when he saw all the baby frogs jumping around.

"Nothing to it!" smiled Iggy. "I shall put them all in this old tin bath while I sunbathe. They'll come to no harm!"

So off went Iggy to sunbathe while all the little frogs simply leapt and jumped and bounced about all over the place.

I think Iggy may need a little help to collect all those bouncing babies, before their mums and dads return!

Don't Say A Word

Lyn and Lucas sat back to back in the garden, not saying a word.

Earlier that day they had been arguing and fighting. Now they refused to speak to one another.

Mother decided not to interfere, and went inside to put her feet up.

So Lyn and Lucas sat looking straight ahead, each one determined not to be the first to speak.

As Lyn gazed up into the sky, a small silver spaceship with a little green man on board circled overhead.

At the same time, Lucas happened to notice a gigantic blue

genie appear from the spout of his dad's watering can.

But Lyn and Lucas sat back to back not saying a word.

Then along came a bright red dragon. It walked right past Lyn, followed by a knight in shining armour.

Was that the Queen in her cloak and crown, strolling on the lawn just in front of Lucas?

But Lyn and Lucas still sat back to back, not saying a word!

Suddenly, out of the long grass, crept a big hairy long legged spider. It ran across Lyn's bare toes and up Lucas's leg.

"Help!" screamed Lyn, jumping in the air.

"Get it off me!" yelled Lucas at the top of his voice.

"Oh good!" said Mother from inside the house. "Lyn and Lucas are speaking to each other at last!"

The Brown Teddy's Wish

"I think it's a shame," sighed the Brown Teddy Bear, "that we can't play with all of the toys when the children have gone to bed."

"But we can!" said Susie the doll. "We play with the bricks and the train, and we do a different jigsaw puzzle every night!"

"She's right!" added the Blue Monkey. "We play in the doll's house and use the tea-set. If you like we can all play 'Snakes and Ladders' tonight!"

"No thanks," sighed the Brown Teddy Bear, and went to sit in a corner by himself.

"I wish we could play in the pedal cars, just like the children!" said Brown Teddy Bear. "Have you seen the way they race around, then crash into each other, with a BANG!"

"We can't do that!" the Blue Monkey replied. "It makes so much noise, it would wake the family.

"I know!" sighed the Brown Teddy Bear, and he went back to sit in the corner again.

However hard they tried, the

82

rest of the toys could not persuade the Brown Teddy Bear to play with them. So night after night he sat alone in the corner.

Then, one day, something happened that changed things. The children who lived in the house came in from the swimming pool and left their blow-up swim rings on the playroom floor.

"What are they for?" asked Susie the doll, are they a new kind of cushion?"

"Not exactly!" smiled the Blue Monkey. "They are full of air, which helps keep you afloat when you're learning to swim."

"They're not a lot of good to us then," remarked Susie the doll, and she ambled off to play dominoes with the finger puppets.

"Now you're quite wrong," said Blue Monkey thinking hard.

"Teddy," he shouted. "Come over here, I want to show you something!" He slipped the swim rings over the pedal cars.

The Brown Teddy Bear's eyes lit up at once. "Now we can race and crash into each other without a BANG!"

"No one will hear us," laughed Susie the doll. "Move over, Teddy, let me have a go!"

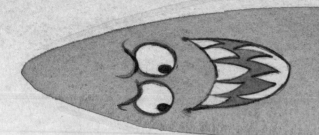

Underwater Fright

Iggy Frog and his best friend Silver Minnow were swimming along in the pond one day, when a long black shadow slowly passed overhead.

"Perhaps it's a duck or a moorhen," said Iggy as he looked round about him.

"Can't be," called Silver Minnow as he darted left and right. "We would have seen their webbed feet!"

All of a sudden Iggy Frog and Silver Minnow looked down, and there was the long black shape swimming beneath them.

"It's a PIKE!" gasped Silver Minnow, and both of them dived behind a rock for safety.

"Pike eat little fish like me!" whispered Silver Minnow.

"And frogs too!" croaked Iggy, quaking with fear.

As soon as the pike disappeared, the two friends swam as fast as they could to the safety of shallow water - for they knew the big pike couldn't follow them there.

"Did you see his sharp teeth?" cried Iggy.

"He's got rows and rows of them," sobbed Silver Minnow. "We'll never be safe in our pond again!"

"Why don't you give that pike the fright of his life?" asked an old water-vole who lived in a hole in the bank.

"How?" cried Iggy and Silver Minnow together.

"Easy!" replied the water-vole. "Paint the underneath of Iggy's yacht to look like a shark. That'll scare him away forever!"

So Iggy fetched his yacht, which was tied up in the reeds, and the two set to work.

As soon as the paint was dry, Iggy, Silver Minnow and the old water-vole launched the boat into the pond and climbed aboard.

"Keep very quiet!" whispered the water-vole as he leaned over the side.

A long black shape sped towards Iggy's yacht. Then, as if by magic, the pike leapt out of the water and across the pond into a nearby stream.

Iggy and Silver Minnow watched him jumping in and out of the water until he was out of sight.

"He's gone for good!" laughed the old water-vole. "We certainly gave him a fright!"

Iggy and the Silver Minnow had to agree!

Paco Goes Shopping

Every Thursday morning, Emilio and his mother and baby sister Maria went shopping.

"My list is very, very long today!" said Emilio's mother with a sigh.

"Perhaps we could carry the shopping home on Paco's back," Emilio suggested.

That morning at the market, Emilio's mother bought lots and lots of shopping.

"Poor Paco will never be able to carry all those bags on his back," said Emilio. "He's far too small."

"Never mind," said his mother. "Paco can carry Baby Maria home, and I'll push the shopping!"

A Weekend Away

The toys had been invited to go to stay in a hotel for the weekend.

"Isn't it exciting!" squealed the dolls, and off they ran to sort out their best clothes.

"How will we get there?" asked the toy dog. "I don't think that any of the other toys have passed their driving test."

"I happen to be a very good driver," said Teddy, who was beginning to feel quite important. "You'll all arrive safe and sound with me behind the wheel!"

The toys were busy all day long washing and ironing their best clothes, and filling their toilet-bags with toothpaste and clean flannels.

A couple of the dolls decided to take their tennis rackets, and the pink rabbit thought it would be a good idea to pack his golf clubs.

"Are we going swimming?" asked the kangaroo.

Teddy thought they probably would go swimming, so all the toys packed their costumes and towels.

First thing next morning, they all gathered on the pavement outside with piles and piles of luggage.

"Oh, my goodness!" gasped Teddy. "There won't be enough room for all of you and your luggage too!"

One or two of the smaller dolls began to cry. "Don't leave us behind Teddy!" they pleaded.

"Now don't be silly," said Teddy kindly. "All of you have brought far too much luggage for just a weekend!"

So Teddy chose the biggest case of all and suggested that the toys just used that.

"This case will fit perfectly on top of the mini-bus, which leaves more room for you all inside."

At first the toys argued about who would take what, but at long last the big case was filled to bursting. The elephant sat on one side and a crowd of toys sat on the other, because that was the only way they could shut the case!

While all this had been going on quite a crowd had gathered. Other toys from down the street had come to see what was going on.

"It's a jumble sale!" one of them shouted to the others.

"No it is NOT!" yelled the rag doll, as she snatched her favourite dress from a big china doll who lived at the bottom of the street.

"Stop arguing and let's get a move on!" shouted Teddy as he walked towards the mini-bus.

"Wait for us!" cried the toys who were busy trying to rescue their belongings.

So the elephant, helped by the pink rabbit, gathered up all the extra clothes and carried them inside the house.

"We'll sort everything out after the weekend," said Teddy as he started up the mini-bus. He looked over his shoulder to check that all the toys had their seat-belts on, and off he went.

The rest of the toys from down the street were left looking rather puzzled as the mini-bus drove away.

Especially when the rag doll stuck out her tongue, and made a rude face at the big china doll who had tried to snatch her favourite dress.

The Robot's Picnic

Ivor had a robot with a very strange name.

"My name is Ivor's Robot!" said the metal man, and that is what he became.

Now Ivor's Robot built himself a puppy. "His name is Spare Part, because that is what he is made of!"

One summer day, Ivor thought it would be a great idea to have a picnic outside under the trees.

"I shall bring the food and set the table," said Ivor's Robot. So off he marched towards the garage where all the tools were kept.

"Have you ever been on a picnic before?" Ivor asked his robot when he looked down at the food on the table.

"No never," said Ivor's Robot, and he shook his head. "I just brought the things I like to eat best and put them on the picnic table!"

So Ivor went inside to the kitchen, and brought out all the food he liked best too, and everyone tucked in and enjoyed the picnic!

Monty's New Village

Monty the Mountie woke up very early in the morning. The night before, lots of animals from the forest had come to stay in his log cabin.

There were so many in fact, that Monty and his new friend the skunk, had to sleep outside.

"I must find the animals somewhere to live," said Monty to himself. "And I must do it before the Chief Mountie pays me a visit. I'm supposed to be keeping a sharp look-out for desperate criminals, not looking after bears and squirrels and beavers... did I say beavers?" All of a sudden Monty had a brilliant idea.

Very gently he woke up a little beaver who had been sleeping in his log cabin.

"Do you have any brothers and sisters?" he asked the little fellow.

"No!" yawned the beaver, still very sleepy. "But I do have lots of aunts and uncles and I don't know how many cousins!"

"Excellent!" grinned Monty. "Let's go and ask them to come over for breakfast."

So before the rest of the animals in the cabin were awake, Monty the Mountie and his little friend set off to find all the other beavers in the forest.

When Monty's jeep pulled up in the clearing by the river where the beavers lived, they had been up for hours. All of them were hard at work felling trees and building a dam.

"You look busy!" said Monty as he wandered over to the Head Beaver.

"Not a bit of it!" the Head Beaver replied. "We've nothing to do when we've finished this dam."

Now when the Head Beaver heard about Monty the Mountie's plan, he was very pleased.

All the beavers were eager to return with Monty and start work straightaway.

"There's nothing a beaver likes better than gnawing through logs all day.

He'll cut down your trees with the greatest of ease.

Give him some wood, and he'll stay!"

91

The beavers sang a song at the tops of their voices as they went back to Monty's cabin.

Now on the way they passed a lumberjacks' camp.

"I'll ask the Chief Lumberjack if I can borrow a bulldozer, and a couple of chainsaws," suggested the Head Beaver. "He's a good friend of mine and we often help each other out."

When at last Monty and the beavers arrived at the log cabin, all the animals were up and dressed and about to have breakfast.

As he tucked into scrambled eggs and toast, Monty the Mountie told them about his plan.

"All of you together, with the beavers' help, are going to build yourselves new homes. First of all we must make a little clearing in the forest, then you can put up your own small village right next to my cabin."

"When do we start?" cried the animals all at once.

"When I've finished my toast!" laughed Monty the Mountie.

The animals began to build their very own village straightaway.

They all worked really hard, and in a while everyone had a home of their own.

No-one was lonely any more, especially Monty the Mountie, who now had lots of new neighbours!